This book belongs to:

_____

Happy Easter Bonnie and Sonny
Love Daddy xx

Fred BLunT

SANTA CLAUS Vs THE EASTER BUNNY

ANDERSEN PRESS

Santa Claus and the Easter Bunny
lived next door to each other.
Santa was a jolly fellow.
Bunny was not.

You see, down in his garden shed, Bunny first had to make the chocolate...

Then fashion the chocolate into eggs...

Then wrap them...
(Even though the foil set his teeth on edge.)

All before delivering them
by himself on foot.

(Which explains why you often
find Easter eggs scattered all
over your garden.)

Bunny didn't have a shiny factory or a workforce of elves.

Keep it up, elves! Only two million toys to go.

Nor did he have a herd of magic flying reindeer to drive him around his delivery route.

And for all his hard work, Bunny never received a single thank you.

Unlike Santa who gets tasty treats from children all over the world.

Milk and cookies in America.

Coffee in Sweden.

Mince pies and sherry in Great Britain.

Rice pudding in Denmark.

And... thank you letters from the kind children of Germany.

Determined to get even with Santa
and those ungrateful children,
Bunny decided to hatch a plan.

He thought...

and thought...

and thought harder still...

until a deliciously
devious plot popped
into his head!

Later that night, the Easter Bunny crept over to Santa's workshop.

He climbed down the great chimney, just like Santa himself, then tiptoed past the silent conveyor belts.

When he got to the merry manufacturing machines,
he pumped them full of warm liquid chocolate.

On Christmas Eve, it was business as usual in Santa's workshop. Almost finished for the year, the tired elves never noticed that the toys were being made of chocolate.

That night, Bunny went to bed early, imagining
Santa racing around the world...

and the sad faces of upset
children as their toys melted
into chocolatey blobs!

At the crack of dawn,
Bunny kicked back
his bedclothes,
ran down
the stairs,

hopped into his
favourite chair,

and switched on
the television.

NEWS JUST IN... MILLIONS OF CHILDREN ALL OVER THE WORLD HAVE WOKEN UP TO FIND ONLY CHOCOLATE TOYS UNDER THE CHRISTMAS TREE. OVER TO YOU CLARISSA GOSSIPA.

THANKS, TREVOR. I'M OUTSIDE THIS FAMILY HOME TO FIND OUT HOW THESE POOR CHILDREN HAVE TAKEN THIS TRULY SHOCKING NEWS...

OH, THIS IS PERFECT. CHILDREN ARE MISERABLE ALL BECAUSE OF NASTY OLD SANTA CLAUS.

I MADE IT ONTO THE HEADLINES!

Bunny was gobsmacked.
Santa was more popular than ever!

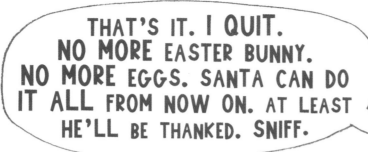

With a heavy heart the Easter Bunny decided to close his workshop and leave town for good.

He was just saying goodbye to his cosy little home when the doorbell rang.

It was Santa Claus!

Bunny didn't like the sound of that.

Before long, Santa had a state-of-the-art chocolate workshop built, complete with chocolate fountain for the sweet-toothed elves.

CHOCLONATOR 2000

Bunny was a happy bunny indeed,
and as for Santa, well, he was always happy.

The End.